My Palace
of
Leaves
in
Sarajevo

Marybeth Lorbiecki

ILLUSTRATED BY

Herbert Tauss

Dial Books for Young Readers
New York

Published by Dial Books for Young Readers
A Division of Penguin Books USA Inc.
375 Hudson Street
New York, New York 10014

Text copyright © 1997 by Marybeth Lorbiecki
Illustrations copyright © 1997 by Herbert Tauss
All rights reserved
Designed by Julie Rauer
Printed in Hong Kong
First Edition
1 3 5 7 9 10 8 6 4 2

Library of Congress Cataloging in Publication Data
Lorbiecki, Marybeth.
My palace of leaves in Sarajevo / by Marybeth Lorbiecki;
illustrated by Herbert Tauss. — 1st ed.
p. cm.
Summary: In 1991, ten-year-old Nadja begins writing to her cousin
in Minnesota, and over the next four years her letters reveal
the horrors of war in this former republic of Yugoslavia,
while her cousin's letters give Nadja and her family some hope.
ISBN 0-8037-2033-5 (trade) — ISBN 0-8037-2034-3 (lib. bdg.)
1. Sarajevo (Bosnia and Hercegovina) — History — Siege, 1992–1996 —
Juvenile fiction. [1. Sarajevo (Bosnia and Hercegovina) — History — Siege,
1992–1996 — Fiction. 2. Cousins — Fiction. 3. Letters — Fiction.]
I. Tauss, Herbert, ill. II. Title.
PZ7.L8766Fr 1997 [Fic] — dc20 96-25933 CIP AC

The illustrations were created with charcoal, oil paints,
and oil crayons on canvas.

This story is based on the published accounts of people living in Sarajevo as well as on stories told to me by Sarajevan refugees.

It is dedicated to my new friends — Samija Mujcinovič and her son, Nedzad; Selma Kusturica-Prcič; Azra Alunovič and Maja Stevanovič; and their families and friends — and to all those valiant souls trying to heal and not hate in Bosnia-Herzegovina and the other regions of the former Yugoslavia. A portion of the proceeds will go to their relief.

This story is also dedicated to Mary, my namesake, who has shown her love for the peoples of the former Yugoslavia. MbL

For my grandchildren —
Ian, Alison, Seth, and Josiah HT

Introduction

Have you ever wondered what it is like to live during a war? How you would eat or wash or run to a friend's?

This is the story of a girl named Nadja who lives in the middle of a war. The war happened not long ago, in the former Yugoslavia—in central Europe, near Italy and Austria and the beautiful Adriatic Sea.

Just as the United States is made up of many states, Yugoslavia was made up of six Communist republics: Slovenia, Montenegro, Macedonia, Serbia, Croatia, and Bosnia-Herzegovina. In the early 1990's some of these republics turned away from communism. They decided they wanted to be democratic nations on their own.

Serbia, the largest republic, did not want Yugoslavia to break up. So it took over the Yugoslav People's Army and invaded Slovenia, Croatia, and finally Bosnia-Herzegovina. This is how the war started.

Nadja's story begins in 1991, just before the war. She lives in Sarajevo, the capital city of Bosnia-Herzegovina. Sarajevo is a city that was famous for its friendliness between people of different religions and backgrounds— "The Spirit of Sarajevo." But as Bosnia moved toward making a new government and breaking away from Yugoslavia, some Bosnians ganged into religious and political groups. When the war erupted, Sarajevans had to decide if they wanted to leave, fight their neighbors, or work to save friendships and hope for peace.

The things Nadja writes of are true.

AUSTRIA

LJUBYANA

SLOVENIA

ZAGREB

CROATIA

BANJA LUKA

BOSNIA-
HERZEGOVINA

ADRIATIC SEA

ITALY

DUBROVNIK

HUNGARY

ROMANIA

N

BOSNIA RIVER

BELGRADE

SERBIA

SARAJEVO

VISEGRAD

MILJACKA RIVER

MONTENEGRO

TITOGRAD

BULGARIA

SKOPJE

MACEDONIA

ALBANIA

GREECE

1991

SEPTEMBER 23, 1991

Pozdravljam te, Alex Chardon,

Do you know you have cousin who is Nadja? This is I. Your father's grandmother is sister of my mother's grandmother, yes?

I live in Sarajevo. I write to you from secret place at top of tree. No one sees me, but I see whole city. It is pretty. Red roofs like hot wafers on white cakes. Minarets and steeples stand tall like soldiers. Everywhere leaves of red and gold and green.

You like to be my friend in post? Then I practice my English. I want to be writer like Father.

I am 10 years old, and I have brother, Denis, he is 4. I call him Dini. I have also fish of many colors. John Wayne is zebra fish. Madonna has tail like swallow. Dini's fish, fast and black, is Mickey.

You write me, yes? Please, molim.

From my palace of leaves in Sarajevo,

Zdravo, *Nadja Didović*

P.S. I send pictures of my family. You send pictures also?

OCTOBER 15, 1991

Dear Nadja,

It's kind of weird to think I have a cousin my age in a place I never heard of. Sure, I'll be your pen pal.

I have a sister who is 13 and BORING! I hope you are more

1

fun than she is. I like soccer and I made a goal last game. Do you play any sports?

We have lots of trees here in Minnesota, but my secret spot's behind some junk in the garage. That's where I keep things away from my nosy sister, Judy. YECH!

Here are some pictures of my family. Judy's the ugly one. Bet you can guess which one is me.

Do you like to ski? I do, but we only have hills here. On the map, I saw you have mountains all around your city. Awesome! Maybe I'll get to see them sometime.

I want to be a forest ranger when I grow up because I love animals.

Your cousin, *Alex Chardon*

P.S. Your English is pretty good. The best I can do is a little Spanish—Adiós! Or should I say Zdravo?

NOVEMBER 21, 1991

Zdravo, Alex,

Zdravo is hello, good-bye, and good things to you.

I LOVE TO SKI, YES! We have beautiful mountains around city. Someday you come, and I show you them. My city is famous place in world for skiing. Very modern. We are hosts for Winter Olympics in 1984. Then I am only 2 years old, but people say it is very thrilling.

I love animals too. My best is birds in my tree. My best person is my friend Ana. She plays football (soccer for you, yes?), basketball, and handball. I do not play sport, but I love to dance. My teacher is gospodja Merkado. She moves as beautiful flower in wind. I want to dance like her. She says she dances to keep Jewish spirit free. Her grandparents put in camps of death by Hitler and Croatian Ustaše. Dances help her not to forget.

I dance because I love it. I have much plans. More choices here now. New government. No communism. Soon we vote to be new country, Bosnia-Herzegovina. No more part of Yugoslavia. We will be more free.

Now we see American movies and we hear music from America and Europe. My best groups are U2 and Crvena Jabuka—Red Apple. What is your best?

Zdravo, *Nadja*

P.S. Thank you for compliments on English. I learn in school. But I tell truth. I use dictionary and Father helps me.

DECEMBER 19, 1991

Hi, Nadja,

I didn't know you had all our music and movies over there. You might think I'm a geek, but I think country music beats everything else. My favorite is Garth Brooks. I want to learn to play the electric guitar so I can be in a country band when I get to high school.

I'm glad things are better in your country now. Dad told me all about Hitler and the Ustashe. He said his grandmother left Yugoslavia because of them.

I don't know much about dancing. Next year in gym we have to take social dance. I don't think I'll like it. Mom says I may change my mind.

It's almost Christmas. Do you celebrate Christmas? Merry Christmas if you do. Here are some Christmas Hershey's kisses for you and your family.

Zdravo, *Alex*

P.S. I like that word, Zdravo. I've tried it on my friends. It's kind of becoming a secret code word with us.

1 9 9 2

Merry Christmas and Happy New Year, Alex!

Hvala for sweet kisses to you and family. We like them much. Dini steal too many. But I try not to be angry at him because it is Christmas — Božić. I have new bicycle and shoes to dance from Saint Nicholas. Happy, happy, happy I am. Big snowflakes are falling now. So soon skijam down mountain!

Winter is beautiful here. But cold. We send packages of care to people in Croatia. We see on TV they are cold and hungry. They are in war. Yugoslav People's Army from Serbia attack them because they want to be their own country.

I hope we never have war here. In Big War, Mother's uncles killed because Serbian. Grandfather's town burned because Muslim. Bad, bad time. Mother and Father worry war come again.

My uncles join Bosnian reserve army. My father not because he has weak heart. (That is how he and Mother meet. She is his doctor.)

Uncles look strange with guns and tree uniforms. Where do we go if war comes?

Zdravo, *Nadja*

P.S. I hope you and family like Bronhi candies and tin of sugary plums.

P.P.S. I do not think you are geek. (That is bad thing, yes?)

Dear Nadja,

Sorry it has taken me so long to write back. I started a bunch of letters, but then I lost them. Those licorices were great! I thought the candied plums tasted okay, but Judy LOVED them. Thank you very much.

I hope it is warmer in Croatia and the war ends soon. My dad was in Vietnam. He says war is one big bloody mess. Sometimes he takes me hunting and I've seen deer and ducks after they've been shot. It kind of makes me sick.

If you're in a war, though, you don't have to worry. Your soldiers will protect you. That's their job.

Do you like camping? Every year my dad and mom take Judy and me up north to go canoeing and fishing. We sleep in a tent and eat around campfires. I love it! I can't wait to go this summer.

Bye for now. I have to write a report on grizzly bears. (I'll need to know about them if I ever become a ranger.)

Alex

APRIL 5, 1992

Zdravo, Alex,

I love to camp! Father writes for outdoors magazines. We camp on Mount Jahorina. We also have holidays by Adriatic Sea. Beautiful!

We have new country now, nation of Bosnia-Herzegovina. SUPER, yes? But two friends close to me, Danica and Gordana, leave city. They say they are Serbian, and they must go because Muslims in power. They think Muslims will hurt Bosnian Serbs because they are Orthodox Christian. Glupo! Stupid! Danica say war is to come, and we must go too because we are Serbian.

I am angry. I am not Serbian only. My father is Muslim. WE ARE BOSNIANS—Sarajevans. Gordana call me half-Turk, balija. How friends can call these mean names to each other? Do people in America care what religion you are?

I think Danica and Gordana wrong about war. Mother says Day of Liberation coming. We celebrate 47 years since end of Big War, end of Hitler and Ustaše.

World never let war come here again. Sarajevo is too famous.

Nadja

A P R I L   1 9 ,   1 9 9 2

Dear Nadja,

Sounds like Gordana and Danica are just jerks who don't know anything. Who needs friends like that anyway?

My mom is part Ojibwe (that's an Indian tribe from northern Minnesota) and part German. Then my dad, he's French and Serbian. So I'm an even bigger mix than you! Kids here don't care what religion you are, but sometimes they ask me dumb questions like "What's it like to be an Indian?" Stupid, huh?

Nothing much is happening here. I'm just waiting for spring. The snow's melting now. I'll be getting my mountain bike out this week if it melts a little more. And in a few more weeks I can go fishing.

Well, Judy's bugging me to take the garbage out before Mom gets home. I'd better go.

Zdravo, *Alex*

APRIL 22, 1992

Dear Alex,

Worst thing in world happen! Yugoslav Army bomb us!!! Last night, big whistles fly down on us and then red-white light and huge thunder explodes and crashes. Pieces of glass and bricks shoot through dark. Everywhere we smell smoke.

Dini screams and not stop crying. We run down to cellar. I shake and shake, and cellar is cold, dark, and smelly. Pound, pound, pound on our ears, for hours, almost forever.

I do not know when I mail this.

Baščaršija, old part of town, has bombs too. We are afraid for grandparents who live there.

GROZNO! HORRIBLE!

I write you when I can. I wish none of this is true.
Nadja

MAY 12, 1992

Dear Alex,

THEY SHOOT AT US!! Soldiers of Yugoslav Army camp in hills on two sides of town like we are big sandwich. They shoot from Trebević Mountain behind our house.

We are not soldiers. Why do they shoot at us? Zašto? Our soldiers fight them, but there are too many.

It is hard to write. Things are very bad. No electricity. Mother is at hospital all time. They close school. Shell hits my teacher and my friends. Sanja, Radovan, Radmila, Sejla. Big explosion, pieces shoot out, hit chalkboard.

Sometimes when close my eyes, I see them with blood.

8

I do not know you can understand. We are alone. Grozno.

I feel like everything squeezed in me. I do not know when all is to come out.

I try to mail this. I am very frightened, very sad. Tužna.
Nadja

P.S. John Wayne, Mickey, and Madonna are dead. No electricity. No bubbles.

M A Y   2 0 ,   1 9 9 2

Dragi Alex,

No letters from you. I hope you write soon. Father says maybe you write but Chetniks in Serbian Army steal letters.

Chetniks turn off water too. Every day Father stands in line to fill jugs at a water pump many streets away. He takes Dini's old stroller to carry. People push store carts, skateboards, carriages for dolls, other things with wheels.

I am afraid for Father all time. Too much work for his heart. Bombs and bullets try to hit him.

We do not watch for him at windows because too much danger.

I take care of Dini. I cook on camp stove.

Do you know how to make bread in tin on stove? I learn how. Father says we pretend that we are hiking on Mount Jahorina. This is good. Soon I have advice for you on camp cooking, yes?

We use candles at night. No TV. One hour radio news with battery.

Run to cellar many times. Bombs, and more bombs. Sit hours and hours.

I miss music!!! I hum and try to dance. Father place

bar for practice in cellar so I stretch while wait during bombs. We bring furniture and books also.

It is difficult to read. Noise is louder than thunder, it shakes me inside.

Father and Dini and I make pretend plays and stories, songs and dances. It is good almost as TV.

But peace, mir, is much better.

Soon it comes? Mir, molim, mir.

Nadja

P.S. No more Olympics for Sarajevo. Beautiful Zetra Hall burned. World forget us now.

JUNE 20, 1992

Dragi Alex,

I am in kitchen. It is dark because we have no glass in windows, only sandbags to stop bullets. Dini draws pictures of sun.

Now we sleep, eat, and take pretend showers with jugs in our kitchen. Other rooms get bullets.

When we go into street, THEY USE US FOR PRACTICE SHOOTING! I stay with Dini in house ALL DAY!!! I miss Ana. Most days, no phone so no friends. BORED, BORED, BORED!

Father tries to make fun. But I know he is afraid. He worries that Mother not come home or that Dini or I be hit by bullets of snipers. These are soldiers who shoot us from hills and tall apartments.

I worry too!!! Ana's mother shot in hip.

When Blue Helmets of United Nations come, we think they are to protect us. But they do not. They watch only,

and soldiers on hill shoot and bomb more, more, more.
Machine guns all night.

Is fun for them?

Nadja

P.S. Mother asks foreign reporter to take my letters out of
Bosnia to send.

J U L Y   6 ,   1 9 9 2

Dragi Alex,

Stores close. All food from black market costs very expensive! Father grows vegetables in suitcases on balcony.
He is very, very fast when he checks them. We have
big jugs to catch rainwater. Sometimes we use water guns
to shoot at plants. Then Mr. Sniper not shoot at us.

Father stands in line 4 hours for UN food. Little tins of
beef and fish, little soap, little oil, little potatoes, rices, and
sugar. It is to last us for long time.

Days are slow and hungry. Do you not think this is
strange way to live? People hope leaders agree to stop
fighting. Every day we think maybe today. Molim.

Nadja

J U N E   2 3 ,   1 9 9 2

Dear Nadja,

We are writing you lots of letters, hoping you will get
one. Maybe this will be the one! Are you alright? Do you
hear gunshots? We have been watching the TV. It looks
horrible!

I asked Dad to tell me about the Vietnam War. But he
wouldn't. Mom says he still gets nightmares. Lately he's

having more of them. He says we should try to help you get out of Sarajevo.

Do you want to come? Write soon and let me know. The other letter is for your dad and mom from my parents.

Love, *Alex*

JULY 10, 1992

Dragi, dragi moj Alex,

Hvala, thank you for your letter. YES, YES, YES, I WANT TO COME!!! I am tired of war. We are prisoners in city. Now only foreign journalists and Blue Helmets and Serbian soldiers use airport and roads out of city. No holidays to mountains or sea. Trapped like zoo animals. No one to bring animals food. Snipers shoot everyone who tries to feed them.

People say you can hear animals cry. They die from hungry. Will we die from hungry?

Mother says WE must leave, but SHE will not. She says she must be here to fix people after shooting and bombs. She seems only little like my mother now. Always tired, always worried.

She must go to hospital on days when shooting stops. Only one car now. We pray no tire go flat on way to hospital, and no accident. People drive fast and crazy to stop snipers from shooting them.

Father does not want to leave Sarajevo without Mother. But he says Dini and I must go. I do not want to leave Mother or Father or my friends.

I do not know what to happen. NAJLJEPŠE HVALA for invite us. THANK YOU, THANK YOU, THANK YOU!

Volim te, love, *Nadja*

Dragi moj Alex,

Urah! Hurrah! I go outside today and we bring Ana!!!
On days not shooting much, Father takes us to parks to
collect grasses and weeds. He does not want us to miss all
summer. Father makes us go, go, go.

We run zigzags. Ana and I keep Dini moving.

Father knows plants to eat from his articles on outdoors. We hang stems and leaves to dry from ceiling in
cellar.

Father tries to teach other people how to do it too. But
they say war MUST be over by winter, it MUST.

Father wishes, but he is not sure. Maybe we come in
America by winter. Do you think? I hope.

I want to run where there is no trata-trata of machine
guns, no thunder that is not with rain, no crash of glass
and bullets flying past.

I want to forget and be little again.

But there is no secret place to go.

Zdravo, *Nadja*

AUGUST 3, 1992

Dragi moj Alex,

It is my birthday—first birthday in war. Father gave
me beautiful bird he carve. Mother comes home and
brings hurmašice—sweet cakes. She gives me pearls Father gave her. She say I am young woman now. I am very
happy to see her. I miss her.

My friend Ana comes and brings me video, Back to the
Future. She trade her best Barbie for it. She says we
watch it when electricity back.

I show her my letter to you and she asks if you are good looking. I say yes, you are relative to me! Many neighbors and friends come to tell Happy Birthday. They bring us water and food so no standing in line today!!! URAH!

Everyone drinks black-market coffee and makes jokes about snipers. We plan ways to trick them. We make pretend people out of rags. We send messages to other buildings with rope to hang clothes. We put things in basket and slide across rope. We flash mirrors with code across streets.

Now I can send messages to Ana even when Mr. Sniper is watching me. Sometimes I am like James Bond spy.

Nadja

P.S. UN has school for us now in different place. People say we must keep living. It is good to be learning new things. I do not want to be glupa, stupid, after war.

SEPTEMBER 30, 1992

Dragi moj Alex,

Do you celebrate saint and angel days? My mother's family does. Today is my angel day. Nadja, name of my angel, means "hope." Maybe I am alive still because my angel is much careful? I do not know.

It is more cold every day. Father says soon we wear our winter underwear and make campfires in our kitchen. Very strange, yes?

No shooting today, so Ana can come to play. Urah!

I hear gospodja Merkado is away. United Nations and

Chetniks let Jewish people leave. Maybe they have places to go. You can not leave unless you are Chetnik or have someone in another country who will take you.

I am so glad America will take us. When will happen? I tire of cards and puzzles and dancing even. I want to see America's trees.

Nadja

Zdravo, Alex,

Mother home for three days! I am so happy! Tomorrow is Dini's birthday. I make him little people out of pieces of wire and paper and old clay. Silly faces, spring bodies.

Mother and I make kolač out of black-market sugar and flour. Then she cut and curl my hair (no hair salon open). I like new hair!!

Mother also help me put many little braids in Ana's hair. Ana says this is good style to play basketball. This night, Ana and me and other friends go to Emir's apartment to watch TV. His father is mechanic and uses car battery for TV.

I learn much about making electricity in this war. Good for science class.

Zdravo, *Nadja*

NOVEMBER 26, 1992

Dragi Alex,

It is so cold, HLADNOĆA! Wind blows between sandbags. UN give us plastic sheets for over windows. It is

little help. Father cut top of my beautiful tree, burn to keep us warm. I am so sad, tužna, tužna. But I thank elm tree for warming us.

Electricity and water on some days, off others. Last month we have none. Dark starts to come at four o'clock. So much time in black. No more candles. We make lamps with jars, oil, and strings from ends of rugs for wicks. We put water in jar so we use less oil.

For radio we listen on little transistor. When batteries wear out, we boil for minutes in salted water and try again.

If electricity or water turns on, even in middle night, we start to work. We sing and joke we are so happy. We fill all containers with water—bathtub, coffeepots, milk jugs, wash buckets, pots, and everything. We wash our clothes and us, and use up little water. We brush teeth with little cup.

All days I dream of BIG TUB with HOT CLEAN WATER for LONG BATH with bubbles!

Nadja

AUGUST 9, 1992

Dear Nadja,

I got a big envelope of your letters. Everything sounds terrible. Why isn't anyone doing anything to stop it all? I don't get it.

Here's a package of some of my favorite stuff. Reese's Pieces, Snickers, licorice, and comic books, markers, a sponge soccer ball and sponge basketball with hoop to use indoors. Mom added a bunch of things she thought you would need. I put in some freeze-dried camping food and

19

my Boy Scout manual too. There are some neat things in there for cooking when you don't have electricity.

My class has all made cards for you and your brother. We saved quarters, and cashed them in for ten-dollar bills. We're sending them in four letters and hoping no one steals them.

Dad has called our government and the United Nations to find out how you can leave. He says it might take awhile. But he's working on it. You will have to tell me all about everything when you get here.

Love, *Alex*

P.S. Please do not think of dying. It scares me.

DECEMBER 23, 1992

Najdraži, dragi moj Alex,

Your package comes. Hvala, Hvala, Hvala!!! It was from heaven. You are from heaven. We are excited too much!!!

I wish you to tell all children in United States to write us letters. They make us SO HAPPY!!! SREĆNA!! We share them with everyone on our street. All neighbors come and my friends—Ana, Elma, Igor, Emir, and Dado.

Does your father think you can help us leave? It is hard for me to think it.

My first best dream is to think of life before war. My second best dream is to leave, maybe come to America.

But not everyone in Bosnia able to come. What of Ana, or Emir, or Igor, or Dado? We plan when older to take car to travel around Europe and go to university, and become famous. It be better if all soldiers go home. Then we be safe.

Your letters and presents make me too happy!! I can not think to write. Thank you thousand billion times.

Blessed PEACE Year, and happy Božić.

You are one of kings who brings gifts.

Love, volim te, *Nadja*

1 9 9 3

Dragi moj Alex,

Many promises of peace! Many lies!! We wait and wait. The leaders change their heads, and we have more war.

I hope you receive letter. We move. Shells are too bad. Our house hit with bomb.

We were in cellar, and I think we are buried forever. Neighbors dig for us while try to stay away from snipers. Long time under earth!!!

We go to live across river with my grandparents near Baščaršija. Sleep on floor in apartment now, but happy I am to be with nana Zada and deda Kemo. Nana sings to us and Deda plays tamboritzan. Old gospodin Romanić in near apartment plays accordion. I dance again.

Mother works all time, and Father is bones and skin. He tries to keep us good feeling and he takes care of old people near us. But at night when he thinks I sleep, I hear him cry. Some refugees from Višegrad tell Father about his sister and her family. Serbian White Eagles attack them. Eagles are very baddest. They do anything. They beat my aunt and uncle, and kill them. Chetniks hurt my cousin, Leila, so many times she feel great pain and shame. She jump out of window to kill herself. Grozno!

Please write and tell me of good things. I am much tired. I miss Ana and other friends. Blocks are too far to visit them.

I give this letter to one Blue Helmet. Many are very kind. They are sad they can not help us more. Some teach us at school.

One man, Hans, from Holland, he leave job for year to be here to help us. How strange! Hans send this to you, I hope.

My heart to you, *Nadja*

P.S. Long time we pray for peace. Now also we pray not to hate.

MARCH 10, 1993

Najdrazi Alex,

No more letters come. Father says that does not mean you write them not.

In night I pretend letters from you. Sometimes Father and Dini do too. Dini's pretend letters are funny. They tell about your neighbors Donald Duck and Mickey Mouse eating much pizza and roast beef and eggs and ice cream.

Most days we eat same things, rices and beans and flour soup with our greens. We have new meal in Sarajevo named "brains." Recipe: fry onions in little oil, add yeast and bread crumbs. I try to make tasty with leaves of plants. But Dini makes funny faces. When I come, I promise to not make experiments for you.

For Ana's birthday, I buy German chocolate bar from black-market sellers—very expensive! But Father says I earn it by helping him carry water and food. I wait for time to visit Ana to surprise her.

It is cold still. Father burns chairs and tables slow as he

23

can to make warm stay longer. It is good Nana makes heavy blankets.

I write again later. I collect letters until I find someone to send.

Volim te, *Nadja*

Dragi moj Alex,

Spring finally here, pretty and warm. I want to fly kite and walk in puddles and play ball in park with Ana.

This spring, birds do not sing. Many trees gone. I visit Ana and see my tree. Cut to stump. My palace of leaves gone forever.

Chetnik leaders and peace people talk and talk. They want to split Bosnia into places for Muslims, Serbs, and Croats. No one in city wants that!!! What will they do with me? Split me in two? Put Ana one place and me in different place? I do not care what my friends are except they are my friends. Most of them are mixes as me. And I miss them. I like it when everyone was together. So many leave because of danger. Some friends lose parents and now run as wild dogs. They turn bad. No food, no home, no love.

I am afraid, afraid, always afraid. What do you do if you are me?

Nadja

P.S. Good Easter to you. Today I must believe more strongly. Sometimes it does not feel like God comes here. Maybe He waits for peace too.

Dragi moj Alex,

I miss your letters. They go to other house, yes? No school, today is Kurban-Bairam. Feast is little. No lamb to eat. Nana and Deda and Father eat no food days before holiday. They eat only in night. (Maybe bean soup and brains taste better in dark!)

Before war, Father does not go often to mosque. Now part of mosque is bombed. Still he goes early morning. Mother takes us more to church also.

I have some new friends. They live in apartment building. Divna and Lada are Serbian. Their families believe in Sarajevo like me. There are many like us. But some people do not trust us now. Tužno. Sad.

Ivana and Elvis are refugees from country. Chetniks kill their parents. Ivana is very quiet. I try to make her smile. Elvis is silly boy. He makes us all laugh.

Robert is nice boy near my age. He plays guitar and has beautiful voice.

Mirna is older, sixteen. She has boyfriend, Dragan. She practices English with me. She wants to be translator someday. She needs to learn computer, but no electricity to use. I want to use computer also. So much to learn.

I try to study more so I not be ignorant when I come to America.

Zdravo, *Nadja*

MARCH 20, 1993

Dear Nadja,

I hope you get this letter. I've written so many, but I don't think you've gotten them.

26

I hope you and your family are still okay. We've been sending packages to you, but I don't think you've been getting those either. We just got your new address, and the Red Cross said they thought they could get this to you.

I made a tape for you of all my favorite songs—with some Garth Brooks and U2 and other stuff. I sent a Walkman with lots of batteries, so you can listen to the tape until you come here.

An immigration lawyer told Dad that he should call our congressman to help us get you and your family visas to get out of Sarajevo. He's tried calling a couple of times but can't get through. He'll keep trying though. I've even written a letter to the President. I hope it helps.

We've been studying the history of your country and the war at school. My friends' families also made care packages and sent them to the Red Cross to hand out.

We all hope this war ends soon too.

Love, *Alex*

P.S. We've been planning our camping trip for this summer, and all I can think of is you.

JUNE 13, 1993

Dear, dear, dragi moj Alex

You and your family much generous. We have package. It is wonderful!!! Izvanredno!! I love tape and Walkman!!! So much I want to give you and your family to thank you.

Hvala for showing world is still good. My heart full to burst with love, I can not write more now.

Nadja

P.S. It is hard, hard, hard to have letters out. Airport closed again. I save until someone to send.

Dear, dragi moj Alex,

Have you wonder ever if you are brave?

Today Father does not come home. He is not home all day. This is not first time.

Every time I feel crazy. This afternoon I start to scream and cry and cry. Nana shakes me to stop. She tells me to write to you.

Can I send bad letter as this? When will Father be home? One time he is missing for many days. Bosnian Army take him to dig trenches. We do not know. So I go with Deda and wagon to stand for water each day. After so, so long, Father comes home.

Maybe today is our turn for death.

I regret such bad letter. I finish later or destroy.

Nadja

P.S. Urah! Urah! God gives us blessing. Father comes home. All day he hides from sniper behind garbage bin. I hate snipers every one.

AUGUST 3, 1993

Dear Alex,

Another war birthday. Mother and Father take me to play, Waiting for Godot. Candles and electric generators light theater. I am proud Sarajevo has plays and music in war. Mother says art keeps spirits alive. Play is not fun, but feels true.

Waiting and waiting. Čekanje.

In apartment we make a little feast of feta cheese and buns from black market and food you send.

At night I go with my friends walking. We stay away from Snipers' Alley. But we do not notice bombs as much now—or shooting. It does not matter where you are. You can be hurt all places. We play guitar and sing songs of Sarajevo. Robert teaches me chords.

I have birthday secret. Maybe Robert likes me. I like him.

What is new for you? Šta ima novo? Please write and tell me of fun things.

Nadja

SEPTEMBER 14, 1993

Dragi moj Alex,

I complain to nana Zada about apartment. UGLY, UGLY, UGLY. Pictures fall from wall and break. Bullet holes and dirt and shelling blasts. Pretty things are sold and furniture burned.

So Nana has party. All people in apartment come. Nana gives us last markers, paints, colors. She tells us to cover walls with happy things. We laugh and sing.

Gospodja Hondo draws stick lady like herself in high heels, dress, red lipstick and nails. She writes, "They can not bomb my dignity" in big letters. She tells us that she says this each morning in mirror. (Chetniks kill her husband.)

Ivana and Elvis draw pictures of parents. Ivana is artist. Her faces like real. Elvis makes cartoons, like Snoopy and Lucy. Elvis is very handsome and sweet.

29

Robert draws band, singing peace songs.

Mirna draws picture of she and boyfriend, Dragan, kissing. Her mother's face red and she stands in front of picture.

But we tease. Then Mirna's mother draws picture of new dress and hat.

Nana draws new shoes.

Deda draws Nana's kolač and pita.

Dini draws guns shooting Chetniks. I am angry. Guns are ugly. I make his guns into vases and holes from bullets into flowers. Then Dini plants tulips in soldiers' heads, and everyone laugh. Me too.

Dini adds yellow motor scooter and pizza. He wants to deliver pizza someday. "But not to Chetniks," he says.

I draw tent on Mount Jahorina for Father, sailboat on Adriatic Sea for Mother, and forest in Minnesota for me.

Urah! We break uglies today!

Nadja

OCTOBER 1, 1993

Dear Alex,

Happy, happy! Electricity on for 4 hours every $2\frac{1}{2}$ days. TV, radio, tapes, and piles of laundry and ironing to do.

Government vote yes on peace plan if all Bosnians can live together. WE CAN!

If peace comes, we try to bring back pretty Sarajevo. Now it is naked. No trees. No birds. Cars and trolleys sit where crashed or shot. Steeples and domes and mosques in pieces. So sad. Tužno.

Maybe it is better someday.

Zdravo, *Nadja*

Najdraži Alex,

Another war winter! No one think we see another. No one think we live through another. I do not believe we can.

There is no heat. It is SO COLD—5 degrees in your measure. Father burns pages from his books. (He saves English dictionary.) All furniture is gone. So are trees and bushes and windowsills and trim.

Sometimes I wonder to die. I hope good smell comes then—something fresh and pretty, like blossoms of cherries, something to make me feel better to leave.

My baka Mara, Mother's mother, soldiers come to her house and tell her they kill her for Muslims hid there. Hvala to God they do not kill. But I miss her. No more visits now. Before war, we see her in summers at farm near Banja Luka. She laugh much and cook good food. (Her baklava best in world!) She and I chase her many goats and chickens.

I want to visit her and chickens. Usamljena, lonely.

Mother is sad much. She works, works, works. Her brother in Belgrade tell her to come home to Serbia. She cries then. She does not write to him again.

Every day we look to last 3 pages of newspaper with dead and wounded names. No more plays for me, or stories, or pretend letters. Too many graves in front of buildings and in park.

Even you can not help us. War is more strong than all of us.

Nadja

Dear Nadja,

I don't know what to write. I didn't send anything in this letter. I just wanted to tell you that I think you're very brave. I wonder what I would do if I were you. I keep thinking about how I'd live without electricity and water and with just a little food. I'm sorry that people you know have been killed or hurt. The only person I knew who died was my grandpa, and I felt really bad.

I feel weird writing about all the fun things happening with me because my life is so easy. But you asked, so I'll try.

I made 2 goals in my soccer game. I earned 3 badges in Boy Scouts. And last week I went camping and canoeing.

I kind of like a girl at school, Andrea. She has pretty red hair and green eyes and cute freckles. She sits next to me in science, so now that's my favorite subject. I'm doing a report on cardinals. They are beautiful red birds. They seem to fly by when good things happen to me. Maybe they are my special animals, kind of like guardian angels. I want my cardinals to fly to you now.

I hope the war ends soon. Dad is still trying to find a way to bring you here.

Zdravo, *Alex*

1994

JANUARY 2, 1994

Happy New Year, Alex!

Thank you for beautiful letter full of feelings. I try to write only good things this year.

Ana gives notes to people going to hospital. Mother brings them home. Ana is funny. She says she tries to learn love poems for times when she will need them.

I have new secret for her and you. Robert draws heart in snow for me. I want to do something for him.

What do boys like? What do you think?

I hope Andrea likes you. I do.

Zdravo, *Nadja*

P.S. I will look for your red birds. (I hope they do not need trees.)

FEBRUARY 6, 1994

Alex, Alex,

In market many bombs cut shoppers—arms and legs and heads. I see blood on stones—68 dead, 200 wounded!

Mother cries and cries. Perhaps she never stop. Father hold her and cry too.

I am so afraid. I hold Dini, but he runs away from me.

I want to run away. Where? Will America ever say we can come?

Nadja

P.S. Sorry for this bad, bad letter.

Urah, Alex!

Dini and I watch UN airplanes fly over us. Big show in air. United States say they bomb guns of Serbian soldiers to stop shelling of us.

I do not believe this is end of war. Chetniks sit on hills to watch us like hunter watches deer. I fear so much bombs come again.

But voices are in street again, no flying hisses in sky. We sled down hill in Lion Cemetery!! (We steer not to hit graves.)

Mother comes home for two days. SUPER! She says she fixed a boy's broke arm. He falls off his sled! She is so happy it is not from war. Mother says that after war is over, she is to find something else to do. She wants to be gardener or painter or something like this.

Father wants to stop gardening, unless it is flowers — just flowers he says, big beautiful flowers of peace!

Dini wants to learn how to ride bicycle, and I want to go to travel and dance and ski.

Thank you, thank you, hvala, for being friend!!!

Nadja

P.S. Olympic President from winter games in Lilleham-mer, Norway, comes to visit. He says world will rebuild Olympic Hall. URAH!!!

P.P.S. Hans goes home to Holland. He says he wishes he can take us with him. He will send my letters to you. Perhaps we come to Minnesota soon, yes?

Dear Nadja,

We worry about you and your family. Mom and Dad packed up some food and warm clothes and candles to help you and your family for the winter. A visa is so hard to get!

Dad heard that maybe your mother could not come here as a refugee because she is a Bosnian Serb. They say she is not under attack. I don't understand it at all. But they say if you and Dini and your father escape to Zagreb, in Croatia, the UN or Red Cross can maybe help get you a plane to Minnesota, and you can stay with us and then send for your mother.

They told us, though, that right now it's too dangerous for your family to try leaving Sarajevo, okay?

We'll ask our senators if they will plead through the UN to have your family flown out, but people say don't count on this happening. Dad says we'll keep trying anyway. We promise!

Love, *Alex*

MARCH 13, 1994

Dear, dear Alex,

Thank you for your packages and letters. So much you give us. Hvala forever. It is happy time for us. Full of HOPE. No more big guns. Not much snipers. Robert and I walk over bridge to see Ana. We play soccer in park with her. Our team won!

On Sunday Bosnia has big soccer game with UN team in broken Olympic stadium. Exciting! Everyone is working to clean up streets and shops. Roads out of city soon open. More food to come! We shall EAT, EAT, EAT!!!

Mirna give me some clothes too little for her. Very fashionable!

So many good things at once! Many good things to you and your family!

Love, *Nadja*

Dear Alex,

It is Mother's saint day, St. Angelina, and we celebrate. We go to cafe on street and we eat pizza and ice cream outside, and we talk to friends who come. Cars go without speed. Everyone walking, SLOWLY, no zigzags!

Mother is at home for holiday, and Father types on old computer again. (Electricity and water work. Urah!) Life feels GOOD again, like clean sheet in spring wind.

I look up to mountains. When Chetniks give us back our mountains, we are free.

I want to teach Dini to ski again. He forgets. He remembers no things but war.

I KNOW I remember. When it is over, I will dance on skis, like thousands of snowflakes. I have many dances in me, waiting for mountains.

When I come to Minnesota, I will show them all to you (even if only on hills).

Nadja

P.S. Mother and Father want us to go from Sarajevo NOW. Father wants to take nana Zada and deda Kemo, but they not go. They say they are too old to be refugees. Father writes papers for us all to leave. We wait for permission. We hope to see you soon.

38

Dear Nadja,

Is it true? Are the leaders really going to make peace? Are things better? I watch the news every night. They say it is. I'm so happy! We are having a party here to celebrate.

I'm glad that Robert likes you too. He must have good taste.

Mom and Dad say that now maybe we can see you soon. I hope so.

Love, *Alex*

P.S. I bet you thought up something nice to do for Robert. I think that if you write him a poem, he'll really like it.

P.P.S. Andrea likes someone else. Oh well.

SEPTEMBER 21, 1994

Zdravo, Alex,

First day autumn. No leaves, because no trees. No permissions to leave. More bombs. I know why symbol of peace is dove. Doves fly away.

Water, gas, and electricity all stop. Chetniks make us puppets. They pull strings, and we stand in lines or run from snipers.

But Father is smart. He takes bicycle and makes little electric generator. We pedal and pedal to listen to radio at night. When we become tired, radio gets quiet. So we call to person on bicycle, "Faster, turn, turn, turn faster."

When spring comes, my family, even Nana and Deda, will be ready for race on bicycles!

I am 13 now. If I live in Minnesota, what do I do at this age? Do I drive car? Do I go to discos? Do I drink coffee at cafes? What movies do you see now? Is rock music same? What do girls wear for new styles?

I feel like I leave world on time machine and go hundred years backward. Bring me to this century, molim.

I miss it.

Zdravo, *Nadja*

NOVEMBER 30, 1994

Dear Nadja,

I've run out of things to write to you. I was so happy when I read your letter about sitting outside at the cafe and eating pizza. But then on the news I hear that the bombing is on again.

I can't believe it! I wish there was something more I could do.

I just keep praying and writing the senators, and sending you letters and packages you usually don't get.

My family and I can help once you get to Zagreb, but we can't get you out of Sarajevo. And we've sent you as many things as we can think of that you might like.

I hope the dark green BOSS shirt is okay. A girl I kind of like named Becca helped me pick it out for you. It's supposed to be big like that.

I like some new bands now—I sent some tapes of them.

Do you think all this will ever end?

Love, *Alex*

1 9 9 5

Dear Alex,

Thank you and your family so much for the money and candles and food and most for beautiful shirt. Hvala also to special Becca.

The dove is with us again. But for how much time?

We want to be free to leave. We are planning again to try to go. I hope soon. I will miss my friends, Ana, Robert, Mirna, and everyone.

But here is cold, so cold. Everyone makes stoves to heat. They push pipes for smoke out windows and walls. Now buildings in city all look like porcupines.

I am tired of no mother. When she is home, we fight. I tell her that she takes care of other people's children, but not hers.

It is bad, I know. But I am feeling bad. I want to leave before peace goes again.

Do you think I am terrible?

Nadja

AUGUST 3, 1995

Nadja, where are you?

How are you? We've called and called the UN and the Red Cross to see if they could find out if you and your family are okay. We haven't heard anything in so long and the news about Sarajevo has all been so bad.

We're hoping you didn't try to escape the city. They say the Bosnian Serbs have been capturing Muslim refugees and killing the men and attacking the women and girls.

IT'S DEMENTED!

I know it is your birthday, Nadja. I'm just praying you and your family are okay. And no, I don't think you are terrible. War is.

I'm so sorry I can't think of anything more to do. Here are some presents for you.

Love, *Alex*

SEPTEMBER 12, 1995

Dear Nadja,

This is just a postcard to ask if you're okay. I'm sending one a week to see if I can get you. Please let us know how you are.

If someone else receives this postcard, please write to us and let us know whatever you know about Nadja Didović and her family.

Zdravo, *Alex Chardon*

OCTOBER 11, 1995

Dear Nadja,

We're still hoping that somehow you and your family are okay and will get this letter. We heard the news today that Sarajevo has gas, electricity, and water!! They say there is a cease-fire and the roads out of Sarajevo will be open soon. If you can, please come right away!

Mom and Dad have wrapped up supplies and money in this package. The Red Cross says they think they can get this to you if you're still in the city. Maybe peace is really coming to stay now that the Chetniks' ammunition piles have been bombed. It has to be over!! It must!! So come now.

   I want to meet you soon, *Alex*

P.S. I know you'll never have your leafy palace back, but here are some acorns and pinecones and elm seeds my friends and I picked. We got as many as we could find. We hope you and your brother can plant them before you leave, so someday when you go to Sarajevo for a visit, you'll find trees and birds back in your pretty city.

NOVEMBER 10, 1995

Dragi, dragi moj Alex,

   I am sorry I do not write to you. My heart was too sick. Tired of bad things.

   Gas line exploded. Dini was hurt. He has to have artificial legs.

   Sometimes I wish explosion hit me. Other times I have thanks it did not.

   Dini tries to make fun. He puts the front wheels of his chair in air and tries to spin. We laugh. But it pains us.

   Mother quit hospital. She says that all this time she heals other people and begs God to protect her family. Now deal is over. She is angry with God.

   I am not angry. I say hvala to God that Dini lives. I know God and his angels save my little brother.

   Father is very quiet. I do not know what he thinks.

   Nana and Deda take care of us now. Every day whole family goes to park with other children and parents of Sarajevo to pray that meetings in America bring peace.

My family leaves here soon. First buses already gone. We wait to hear if they pass Chetniks without danger. Jewish Center help us join convoy out of city. Nana and Deda come also.

Ana and her family want to stay. She is brave. I will miss her and my pretty city. Father says we give all we have to Sarajevo. We try to keep it place for all kinds of people, to keep our hope in war. Maybe now different people must build city again.

Thank you for birthday gifts and all many gifts. Most precious to me are seeds for trees. Dini and I will plant them before ground freezes. We will go to our old house and plant elm seeds in hole where my tree was.

Maybe one will grow.

Nadja

"Sarajevo is everything I am dreaming of every day."

—Maja Stevanovič, sixteen-year-old Sarajevan
now living in America

Afterword

In 1995, shortly after this story ends, peacekeeping troops arrived in Bosnia-Herzegovina. Since that time, food has become more available, as well as gas, water, and electricity. Once again people have been able to try to rebuild their homes, shops, schools, and lives. Gradually most of the roads have been reopened so Sarajevans can now come and go more easily—even to Nadja's mountains. Still, it will take a long time for all the people of Bosnia to heal.

This is in part because the war was not waged just against soldiers, but against civilians. More than 11,800 people have been killed in Sarajevo alone, 1,500 of them children. Many more have lost arms and legs, mothers and fathers, brothers and sisters, their homes.

As the Jewish people were targeted by Hitler in World War II, people of Islamic belief or Muslim descent have been targeted in this war. This policy has come to be called "Ethnic Cleansing." Thousands upon thousands of Muslims have been slaughtered, tortured, or put into concentration camps. Over 1,000 mosques have been destroyed; few if any remain standing in the territories taken by the Bosnian Serbs and the Yugoslav People's Army. Many of these army units have specifically attacked women and children. Schools and hospitals have been bombed, school buses kidnapped, women and girls raped.

How could neighbors do this to neighbors? Part of the answer lies in World War II. During that war, three different groups fought for control in the Yugoslav area: the Croatian Ustashe (who worked with Hitler), the Serbian Chetniks, and the Communist Partisans. The Muslims did not fit easily with any group because they were neither Catholic like the Croatians, nor Orthodox Christian like the Serbians. Nor did they all believe in communism. So some tried not to take sides. Others worked with the Ustashe, or fought with the Partisans against both the Ustashe and the Chetniks. Many Muslims were killed. In the end the Communist Partisans were on the winning side of the war, and they brought all the groups together under one Communist government. But many Serbians in Bosnia never forgave the Muslims for not rising up as a group against the Ustashe.

When the democratic elections took place in Bosnia in 1990, some of the major parties had their roots in the same groups that fought in World War II. There was a Communist party, a Bosnian Croatian party, and a Bosnian Serb party. But the party that won the leading role in the new Bosnian government was the Party of Democratic Action, which had a majority of Muslim members. This election victory outraged members of the Bosnian Serb party. So when the Yugoslav People's Army invaded Bosnia, the Bosnian Serbs fought along with them (and later kept the war going on their own).

Throughout the days of elections and political arguments, most Sarajevans tried to keep the city's spirit of unity alive. On April 5, 1992, the day the shooting began in the city, thousands of people marched in the streets chanting, "Bosnia! Bosnia! We can live together!"

Unfortunately the war changed Sarajevo. Many people left, especially Bosnian Serbs. And a large number of refugees from the Bosnian countryside came to the city bringing with them no memory of the friendliness between peoples that once thrived there. Still, many Sarajevans who chose to stay throughout the war want their old city back—a place where all are welcomed, all live in peace. Perhaps in time, as war criminals are imprisoned and angers die down, they will prevail and the Spirit of Sarajevo will return.

Nadja means hope.

Glossary and Pronunciation Guide

baka [**bahk** hah] — Grandma (often used by Christian Bosnians).

baklava [**bahk** lah vah] — A multilayered nut pastry.

balija [bah **lee** yah] — A nasty name meaning "stupid Muslim fool."

Bašcaršija [Bahsh **char** shee yah] — Name of historic Turkish-style market in the middle of Sarajevo's downtown, in a traditionally Muslim area of the city.

Bosnia-Herzegovina [**Bohz** nee ah-**Her** tzeh goh vee nah] — One of the republics of the former Yugoslavia, now recognized as a nation by the United Nations.

Božić [**Boh** zheetch] — Christmas.

Bronhi [**Brohn** hee] — Brand of licorice candies.

čekanje [cheh **kahn** yeh] — Waiting.

Chetniks [**Cheht** neeks] — The Serbian troops fighting the Ustashe, Muslims, and Nazis in World War II. Later it became a nasty name for Serbians who were disliked. During the war in the 1990's the *Chetniks* were the Serbian troops, whether part of the troops of the Yugoslav People's Army or the army of the Bosnian Serbs.

deda [**deh** dah] — Grandpa (often used by Muslim Bosnians).

dragi [**drah** gee] — Dear; *dragi moj* [**drah** gee moy] — My dear.

glupo, glupa (feminine form) [**gloop** oh, **gloop** ah] — Stupid.

gospodja [goh **spoh** jah] — Mrs.; *gospodin* [goh **spoh** deen] — Mr.

grozno [**grohz** noh] — Horrible.

hvala [**hvah** lah] — Thanks, or thank you.

hladnoća [**hlah** dnoh tchah] — Cold.

hurmašice [hoor **mahsh** ee tseh] — A sweet cake.

izvanredno [eez **vahn** rehd noh] — Wonderful.

kolač, kolači (plural) [**koh** lahch, **koh** lahch ee] — Cake(s).

mir [meer] — Peace.

moj [moy] — My.

molim [**moh** leem] — Please.

Nadja [**Nah** djah] — Hope in Russian (name brought into Bosnia through connection to Russia and Eastern Orthodox Church).

najdraži [**nahyeh** drah zhee] — Dearest, or most dear.

najljepše [**nahyeh** lyehp sheh] — Most beautiful.

nana [**nah** nah] — Grandmother (often used by Muslim Bosnians).

pita [**pee** tah] — A rolled pastry filled with meat, cheese, or spinach.

pozdravljam te [**pohz** drah vlyahm teh] — Greetings to you.

skijam [**skee** yahm] — I am skiing.

srećna [**sretch** nah] — Happy.

Šta ima novo? [**Shtah ee** mah **noh** voh?] — What's new? What's up?

tužno, tužna (feminine form) [**too** zhnoh, **too** zhnah] — Sad.

urah [oo **rah**] — A cheer, hurrah.

usamljena [oo **sahm** lyeh nah] — Lovely.

Ustaše [Oo **stah** sheh] — The fascist Croatian government in World War II that was known for its terrorizing of anyone who stood in its way of killing Jewish, Romani (gypsy), and Serbian peoples.

volim te [**voh** leem teh] — I love you (not romantic).

zašto? [**zahsh** toh] — Why?

zdravo [**zhdrah** voh] — Hello, good-bye, good things to you.

The Bosnian-Serbian-Croatian language is complex. The language has two written forms — one using the Roman alphabet and favored by those of Catholic or Croatian heritage; the other using the Cyrillic alphabet and favored by those of Orthodox Christian or Serbian heritage. In Bosnia, both are in use. In Sarajevo, people were so comfortable with the two alphabets that one of the city's major newspapers, *Oslobodjenje* (*Liberation*), would publish one day in Roman and the next in Cyrillic, to be fair to all. As the war developed and the people of Sarajevo became angrier and angrier with the Serbian armies shelling them, the paper started to publish only in Roman.

Acknowledgments

I am thoroughly indebted to Zlata Filipović, the young Sarajevan woman who wrote *Zlata's Diary*, 1994; to Zlatko Dizdarević, who wrote *Sarajevo: A War Journal*, 1993; to Dzevad Karahasan, who wrote *Sarajevo, Exodus of a City*, 1994; to Tom Gjelten, who wrote *Sarajevo Daily: A City and Its Newspaper Under Siege*, 1995; and to Fred Singleton, who wrote *A Short History of the Yugoslav Peoples*, 1985.

Special thanks also to all the other valiant journalists and photojournalists who risked their lives to bring us the voices, faces, and stories of the people of ex-Yugoslavia, most specifically to those who prepared the National Public Radio interviews with the people of Bosnia. It was these interviews which made me realize with my heart that there were individuals, not just numbers of people, being hurt in this "civil war."

For assistance in authenticity, accuracy, and manuscript preparation, I want to thank Editor Diane Arico; Professor Vanča Schrunk, who teaches the Serbo-Croatian-Bosnian language and works with Bosnian refugees; Cheryl Robertson, nurse at the Center for Victims of Torture, Minneapolis; Thomas Kosell of Catholic Charities; the Minneapolis Public Library; Muriel Dubois and her writers' circle; Heidi and Fr. Nathan Kroll of the Eastern Orthodox Christian faith; Hesham Reda from the Islamic Center of Fridley; Jill Anderson, Lori Schaefer, Mary Beth Nierengarten, Jean Lorbiecki Nelson, LeAnn Lorbiecki, and Danny McAdam; and last but not least, for their encouragement and support, my husband David Mataya, agent Edythea Ginis Selman, and Lillian Lent.

In the journey of writing this book, I have been most enriched by the new friendships it has brought me. I want to extend my heart in gratitude to the many wonderful people of different heritages from Sarajevo and the former Yugoslavia who have assisted and befriended me: Samija, Nedzad, and Selma; Maja and Azra and their families; Zaim and Zada; and the glue that holds us all together: Mirjana Bijelić and Boris Kalanj.

For readers who would like to write letters or send care packages to children in Bosnia or in Bosnian refugee camps, call or write:

The United Nations High Commissioner for Refugees
1 U.N. Plaza
Room 2610
New York, NY 10017
(212) 963-0032

The U.S. Committee for UNICEF*
333 East 38th Street
New York, NY 10016
(212) 686-5522

Care packages might include a personal note and/or photograph. The children can use items such as books, school supplies, soap, toothbrushes and toothpaste, underwear, T-shirts, and toys.

In addition, there may be refugees from the former Yugoslavia living near you who would like to make new American friends. For information, call the Catholic Charities, Lutheran Social Services, or Islamic Center nearest you.

*This organization will accept money (checks or money orders only), not care packages, but readers can specify where they would like donations to go.